D0413213
Read Me to Sleep
This book belongs to ...

Read Me to Sleep™

How to use this story to help ease your child to sleep

1 PREPARE. After reading these instructions and before reading to your child, listen to a sample of the story being read aloud at this link: **www.readmetosleepbooks.com**. Follow along with the text and notice the pace, the pauses and the emphasis on certain words, as well as the extended vowel sounds. You may want to read the text aloud by yourself at first to ensure the extended vowel sounds and unnaturally slow reading pace become comfortable. After practising several times, you may want to adapt word emphasis to fit your own rhythms.

2 SHARE. When you're ready for a nighttime reading, let your child browse through the book and enjoy the pictures first, so he or she can imagine them as you read the story aloud. This should be the last story read at bedtime; it is encouraged that you read other favourite laptime or bedtime stories prior to this book. At this point in your bedtime routine, your child should be ready to relax in a resting position, and close his or her eyes.

3 RELAX AND BREATHE. Before you start the story, take several deep, cleansing breaths and encourage your child to do so along with you. Breathing is a key relaxation technique used in Read Me to Sleep. It's recommended to inhale through the nose and exhale through the mouth audibly, with the exhalation twice as long as the inhalation. This will force you and your child to take deeper, calming breaths.

4 READ THE STORY ALOUD. In a slow, gentle voice, follow the reading cues suggested:

- You may choose to replace the **green** words with objects (or people) from your child's life that are meaningful and provide comfort.
- When you encounter **blue** words, stretch out the primary vowel sound in each word.
- Read the **purple** words in a hushed voice or a whisper.
- Line breaks demonstrate where you should pause briefly, with ellipses demonstrating a longer pause.

5 RETURN TO THE BEGINNING. If your child is not asleep by the end of the story, simply maintain your rhythm and begin the text again without telling the child that the story has ended. The repetition and cyclical pattern are calming, and the story should feel like an endless entry into sleep.

ORCHARD BOOKS
First published in Great Britain in 2016 by The Watts Publishing Group

1 3 5 7 9 10 8 6 4 2

Cover design by Elliot Kreloff

A CIP catalogue record for this book is available from the British Library.

ISBN 978 1 40834 549 8

Printed and bound in China

Orchard Books
An imprint of Hachette Children's Group
Part of The Watts Publishing Group Limited
Carmelite House
50 Victoria Embankment
London EC4Y 0DZ

An Hachette UK Company

www.hachette.co.uk

www.hachettechildrens.co.uk

Let's Go to Sleep

By Maisie Reade
Illustrated by Laura Huliska-Beith
Afterword by Dr James B. Maas

NOTE FOR READER: *You may replace 'Little Fawn', 'Tiny Squirrel', 'Cosy Bear', and 'Lazy Lion' with the names of real toys, dolls or friends. When you encounter blue words, stretch out the primary vowel sound. The words in purple can be said in a hushed voice or a whisper. After the words 'breathe in' and 'breathe out', demonstrate those actions for your child by taking a deep breath in and letting a deep breath out, as described on the first page.*

Take my hand, little child,
and follow this winding path
to the Forest of Dreams.
Here the air is magic
that you breathe in …
and breathe out.
It fills every part of you with your very best dreams
that send you right to sleep with a smile.
The way is lit by warmly glowing fireflies,
and a gentle breeze carries a scent of pine
that you breathe in …
and breathe out.

Before you can say "sleepytime", you've arrived!
See? You're surrounded by all of your friends,
like Little Fawn and Tiny Squirrel
and Cosy Bear and even Lazy Lion.
They're on the very same journey that you are …
the journey to dreamland.

Mama Bird welcomes you to the Forest of Dreams.
"Take off your shoes and get cosy.
You'll be here awhile," she tells you.
Go ahead …
The ground is cool **and soft on your bare feet**
like a sandy beach at twilight,
and your toes sink in just **right.**

Then, Mama Bird tells you a very **important secret:**
If you know how to breathe**,**
you know how to sleep.
It's true! If you know how to breathe**,**
you know how to sleep.
After the word 'sleep', inhale and push a complete breath out through the mouth.

Mama Bird is the only **animal in this forest**
who stays awake through the dawn.
She watches over the others all **night long,**
and is always **sure that they're safe.**

When you encounter blue words, stretch out the primary vowel sound. The words in purple can be said in a hushed voice or a whisper.

'Little Fawn' may be replaced with a favourite animal, toy, doll or friend. The other items mentioned may be replaced with objects that comfort your child. When you encounter blue words, stretch out the primary vowel sound. The words in purple can be said in a hushed voice or a whisper.

Little Fawn is here, too, but Little Fawn isn't sure what to do.
She thinks she needs *things* to put her to sleep.
Little Fawn says,

"Mama Bird, I'm here, and I'm ready for sleep.
Mama Bird, can you bring my warm, furry blankie?
Mama Bird, can you bring my fluffiest pillow?
Mama Bird, can you bring my favourite little sparrow,
so I may hear her sweet songs?
Mama Bird, can you bring my softly glowing night-light?
I am so tired, so very tired.
I am ready for sleep ...
so ready for sleep."

Take a deep breath in and exhale audibly before turning the page.

You may choose to replace 'blankie' with another favourite comforting toy, doll or item. When you encounter blue words, stretch out the primary vowel sound. The words in purple can be said in a hushed voice or a whisper. You may also yawn along with Little Fawn when it is mentioned.

Mama Bird nods, and says,
"You could climb on my back
and we could look for your blankie.
We could fly high and low, to the tips of the treetops ...
then dip down below - sailing into the hollows ...
into burrows and tree nooks and nests."

Little Fawn gives a yawn.
"I'd like that," she responds.
Ready to fly, she trots over to Mama Bird.

Mama Bird shakes her head with a smile.
"We could look for your blankie, Little Fawn,
but you don't need your blankie ... you don't need it at all.
The air in this forest is all that you need.
It's everywhere around you ...
and everywhere inside you.
It's filled with magic that allows you to sleep.
So breathe deep and dream, Little Fawn,
breathe deep and dream!"

When you encounter blue words, stretch out the primary vowel sound. The words in purple can be said in a hushed voice or a whisper. You may choose to incorporate the interactive breathing into the storytelling, as shown in the notes below, or wait until the bottom of the page to breathe together, based on what works best for you and your child. Guidance for your child may be needed for the first several reads.

Mama Bird flutters her wings,
encouraging Little Fawn to come to rest.
"First you lie down, then close your eyes," she says.
"Take a long breath in and count to three …
so the air reaches all the way to your toes!
There it goes!
You may choose to prompt your child here by adding: 'Breathe in … 1 … 2 … 3 … !'

"Hold your breath so it stays inside - just a few more seconds,
so your whole body is ready to fall asleep.
When you feel the magic tingle on the tips of your toes,
let out your breath, Little Fawn, until there's nothing left."
You may choose to prompt your child here by exhaling audibly with a 'whoosh' sound for a count of six: 'Whoooooooooosssssssh!'

Tiny Squirrel is still awake and scampers over.
Mama Bird tucks the little creature under her soft wing, and says,
"Let's breathe in together now, with all of your friends,
so we can help Tiny Squirrel fall asleep, too."

Now encourage your child to breathe in, hold the breath, and breathe out along with you, as described on the first page.

Little Fawn gives a yawn.
"You're right, Mama Bird. I don't need my blankie.
Can we find my fluffiest pillow instead?
I am so tired, so very tired.
I am ready for sleep …
so ready for sleep."

Mama Bird nods, and says,
"You could climb on my back and we could look for your pillow.
We could fly here and there - to mountains and peaks,
to valleys and rivers, and soar far over meadows
into caves and canyons and dens."

Another yawn from Little Fawn.
"What an adventure!" She sighs. "I'd love to go."

You may yawn and sigh along with Little Fawn. When you encounter blue words, stretch out the primary vowel sound. You may also choose to replace 'blankie' and 'pillow' with other comforting objects from your child's world. The words in purple can be said in a hushed voice or a whisper.

You may choose to incorporate the interactive breathing into the story, as shown in the notes below, or wait until the bottom of the page to breathe together.

Mama Bird shakes her head with a smile.
"Oh, but you don't need your pillow ... you don't need it at all.
The air in this forest is all that you need.
It's everywhere around you, and everywhere inside you.
It's filled with magic that allows you to sleep.
If there's one thing you need, you need to breathe deep.
Take a long breath in and count to two,
so your belly inflates, just like a balloon!
You may choose to prompt your child here by adding: 'Breathe in ... 1 ... 2!'

"Now hold your breath so it stays inside - just a few more seconds,
so you feel the magic swirl right up to your heart.
Then let out your breath, Little Fawn, until there's nothing left."
You may choose to prompt your child here by exhaling audibly with a 'whoosh' sound for a count of five: 'Whoooooooooossssssssh!'

Cosy Bear is still awake and lumbers over for a hug.
Mama Bird's wings are open so wide,
they reach all the way around the drowsy cub.
"Let's breathe in together now, with all of your friends,
so we can help Cosy Bear fall asleep, too."

Now encourage your child to breathe in, hold the breath, and breathe out along with you, as described on the first page.

You may choose to replace 'blankie,' 'pillow,' and 'sparrow' with other comforting objects or pets from your child's world. When you encounter blue words, stretch out the primary vowel sound. The words in purple can be said in a hushed voice or a whisper. You may also sigh along with Little Fawn.

Little Fawn's eyes start to fall shut.
"You're right, Mama Bird. I don't need my blankie or my pillow.
But can we look for my favourite little sparrow,
so I may hear her sweet songs?
I am so tired, so very tired.
I am ready for sleep … so ready for sleep."

Mama Bird nods, and says,
"You could climb on my back
and we could look for your sparrow.
We could search far and wide … beyond the wood's edge,
over the ocean, then touch the horizon
to the north, and the south, and the east and the west."

Little Fawn opens one eye.
"Yes, let's!" she says with a sigh. "I'd love to go."

Mama Bird shakes her head with a smile.
"Oh, but you don't need your little sparrow … you don't need her at all.
The air in this forest is all that you need.
It's everywhere around you, and everywhere inside you.
It's filled with magic that allows you to sleep.
So breathe deep and dream, Little Fawn,
breathe deep and dream!

When you encounter blue words, stretch out the primary vowel sound. The words in purple can be said in a hushed voice or a whisper. You may choose to incorporate the interactive breathing into the story, as shown in the notes below, or wait until the bottom of the page to breathe together.

"Take a long breath in
so the air can reach all the way to your fingertips.
You may choose to prompt your child here by adding: 'Breathe in deep!'

"Hold your breath so it stays inside - just one more second,
so your fingers are tingly, and ready to sleep.
Then push out your breath, Little Fawn, until there's nothing left.
Keep going, keep going ... "
You may choose to prompt your child here by exhaling audibly with a 'whoosh' sound for a count of four: 'Whoooooooooossssssssh!'

Lazy Lion is here, too, and she rolls over on her back for a belly rub.
Mama Bird tickles her tummy with the tips of her wings, and says,
"Let's breathe in together now, with all of your friends,
so we can help Lazy Lion fall asleep, too."

Now encourage your child to breathe in, hold the breath, and breathe out along with you, as described on the first page.

Little Fawn gives a yawn.
"You're right, Mama Bird.
I don't need my blankie, my pillow, or even my little sparrow.
But can we look for my night-light? Or maybe the moon?
I am so tired, so very tired.
I am ready for sleep …
so ready for sleep."

Mama Bird nods, and says,
"You could climb on my back and we could look for the moon.
We could fly to the clouds … and even to space.
We could sail past the sun and the planets and stars
and then we could make our way home."

Little Fawn is almost asleep now, and she knows the secret.
"We'll come home because I don't need light tonight.
I don't need it at all.
The air in this forest is all that I need.
It's everywhere around me
and everywhere inside me.
It's filled with magic that allows me to sleep.
If there's one thing I need, I need to breathe deep."

You may yawn along with Little Fawn. You may choose to replace 'blankie', 'pillow', 'sparrow' and 'night-light' with other comforting objects or pets from your child's world. When you encounter blue words, stretch out the primary vowel sound. The words in purple can be said in a hushed voice or a whisper.

When you encounter blue words, stretch out the primary vowel sound. The words in purple can be said in a hushed voice or a whisper.

Mama Bird smiles and nods.
"You're right, Little Fawn.
You don't need your blankie or your pillow,
your little sparrow or your night-light or even the moon.
You're so very tired; you're ready for sleep.
You want to go to sleep!

"Take one more breath in
so the air fills you all the way up ...
from your toes to your belly to your heart ...
then out to your fingers and up to your head!
When you feel the magic tingle all the way to your hair,
push out your breath, Little Fawn, until there's nothing left.
Whooooooooooossssssh!"

If your child is still fully awake, he or she can now be prompted to breathe in, hold the breath, and breathe out along with you, as described on the first page.

You may replace the characters with names of favourite toys, dolls or friends. When you encounter blue words, stretch out the primary vowel sound. The words in purple can be said in a hushed voice or a whisper.

And when you enter dreamland, dear child,
there is no better place to be tucked in
than the Forest of Dreams,
where Little Fawn and Tiny Squirrel, Cosy Bear and Lazy Lion,
and all of the other creatures are curled up tight …
and Mama Bird is awake all night watching over every creature,
making sure they are comfy, making sure they are safe.
Tomorrow night there will be a new little creature in the forest,
and you'll know exactly what to tell her, won't you?

You'll say,
"Take my hand, my friend,
and follow this winding path
to the Forest of Dreams.
Here the air is magic
that you breathe in …
and breathe out.
It fills every part of you with your very best dreams
that send you right to sleep with a smile."

Breathe deep and dream, my friends,
breathe deep and dream!

Return to the beginning if your child is not yet asleep.

A prescription for great sleep tonight ... for a better tomorrow!

By Dr James B. Maas founder of Sleep for Success, and author of the *New York Times* bestseller *Power Sleep*.

The science of sleep medicine has determined unequivocally that sleep is fuel for the brain. It is critical for physiological, emotional and cognitive development that will affect your child's entire life span. It is never too early to establish good sleep practices for your child - routines and strategies that ensure effective daytime performance, good health and general well-being - especially since sleep habits can often be difficult to change once established.

Preparing for healthy sleep

Every child should get proper mental and physical exercise during the day. Make sure your child maintains a balanced diet. Avoid chocolate, sweets and sugary drinks after 2 p.m., and mealtimes and snacks should not be scheduled too close to bedtime. Make sure the bedroom is quiet, dark and cool and provide a good pillow and mattress.

Steer clear of stimulation before bedtime

Avoid heavy exercise or energetic activity within an hour of bedtime. Activities like watching videos stimulate children and keep them tossing and turning at night. Furthermore, the blue daylight spectrum light from TVs, iPads, video games and computer screens blocks the flow of melatonin and delays sleep onset.

Develop a bedtime routine

Ensure that your child goes to bed and gets up at the same time every day. As soon as your child is about three to four months old, it's vital to develop an age-appropriate sleep schedule and to stick to it! Children with consistent schedules are better rested and easier to manage at bedtime because their bodies are trained to sleep and wake at certain times.

You should devise a bedtime routine that's about thirty minutes long and includes soothing activities, such as taking a bath and reading. These activities will help calm your child and relax the nervous system. The best activity to facilitate sleep onset is using good breathing techniques. Read Me to Sleep stories apply these findings of scientific research to enable your child to reap the benefits of body and brain relaxation at bedtime.

Reinforce good sleep habits

Provide positive reinforcement. Reward your child for following bedtime rules and staying tucked in at night. Give a sticker for every successful night, and when ten stickers are earned, award a small prize or privilege. Offer praise for cooperation.

And that goes for you, too!

By ensuring that you're well rested and healthy, you're being the best caregiver you can be. Learn to value your own sleep. Sleep is not a luxury; it's a necessity. Set a good example for your child, and you'll both be rewarded with a great, wide-awake life.

James B Maas